A Note to Parents and Teachers

Kids can imagine, kids can laugh and kids can learn to read with this exciting new series of first readers. Each book in the Kids Can Read series has been especially written, illustrated and designed for beginning readers. Humorous, easy-to-read stories, appealing characters, and engaging illustrations make for books that kids will want to read over and over again.

To make selecting a book easy for kids, parents and teachers, the Kids Can Read series offers three levels based on different reading abilities:

Level 1: Kids Can Start to Read

Short stories, simple sentences, easy vocabulary, lots of repetition and visual clues for kids just beginning to read.

Level 2: Kids Can Read with Help

Longer stories, varied sentences, increased vocabulary, some repetition and visual clues for kids who have some reading skills, but may need a little help.

Level 3: Kids Can Read Alone

Longer, more complex stories and sentences, more challenging vocabulary, language play, minimal repetition and visual clues for kids who are reading by themselves.

With the Kids Can Read series, kids can enter a new and exciting world of reading!

Franklin and the Tin Flute

From an episode of the animated TV series *Franklin*,
produced by Nelvana Limited, Neurones France s.a.r.l. and
Neurones Luxembourg S.A, based on the Franklin books
by Paulette Bourgeois and Brenda Clark.

Story written by Sharon Jennings.

Illustrated by Céleste Gagnon, Sasha McIntyre, Robert Penman and Laura Vegys.

Based on the TV episode *Franklin's Family Treasure*, written by Patrick Granleese.

Kids Can Read ™ Kids Can Read is a trademark of Kids Can Press Ltd.

Franklin is a trademark of Kids Can Press Ltd.
The character of Franklin was created by Paulette Bourgeois and Brenda Clark.
Text © 2005 Context*x* Inc.
Illustrations © 2005 Brenda Clark Illustrator Inc.

Kids Can Press acknowledges the financial support of the Government of Ontario,
through the Ontario Media Development Corporation's Ontario Book Initiative; the
Ontario Arts Council; the Canada Council for the Arts; and the Government of
Canada, through the BPIDP, for our publishing activity.

Published in Canada by
Kids Can Press Ltd.
29 Birch Avenue
Toronto, ON M4V 1E2

Published in the U.S. by
Kids Can Press Ltd.
2250 Military Road
Tonawanda, NY 14150

www.kidscanpress.com

Series editor: Tara Walker
Edited by Yvette Ghione
Designed by Céleste Gagnon

Printed and bound in China

The hardcover edition of this book is smyth sewn casebound.
The paperback edition of this book is limp sewn with a drawn-on cover.

CM 05 0 9 8 7 6 5 4 3 2 1
CM PA 05 0 9 8 7 6 5 4 3 2 1

Library and Archives Canada Cataloguing in Publication

Jennings, Sharon
      Franklin and the tin flute / Sharon Jennings ; illustrated by
Céleste Gagnon ... [et al.].

(Kids Can read)
The character Franklin was created by Paulette Bourgeois and
Brenda Clark.

ISBN 1-55337-800-8 (bound). ISBN 1-55337-801-6 (pbk.)

I. Gagnon, Céleste II. Bourgeois, Paulette III. Clark, Brenda IV. Title. V. Series: Kids
Can read (Toronto, Ont.)

PS8569.E563F7175 2005   jC813'.54   C2004-904712-4

Kids Can Press is a *l*⊙*ᴦ*U*S* ™ Entertainment company

Franklin and the Tin Flute

Kids Can Press

Franklin can tie his shoes.

Franklin can count by twos.

And Franklin can play the triangle
and the tambourine.

But Franklin cannot play a tin flute.

So when Franklin found a tin flute,
he gave it away.

Now, Franklin needs it back.

One day, Franklin was playing

in the basement.

He found an old box.

Inside was a tin flute.

Franklin picked it up and blew.

Twack!

"Ugh," said Franklin.

He blew the flute again.

Toot! Tweak!

"Hmmm,"

said Franklin.

"Maybe I will get

better with practice."

Franklin played the flute
all morning.

Toot! Toot! Tweak! Tweak!

"Hmmm," said Franklin.

"I am not getting better.

I am getting *worse!*"

Franklin went to the park.

On the way, he blew the tin flute

again and again.

Twack! Toot! Tweak!

Tweak! Toot! Twack!

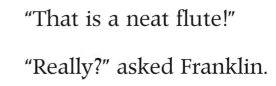

"Wow!" said Rabbit.

"That is a neat flute!"

"Really?" asked Franklin.

"I'll trade you for it,"

said Rabbit.

He held out his best,

green marble.

"It's a deal!"

said Franklin.

At lunchtime, Franklin showed everyone

his marble.

"I got it from Rabbit," he said.

"I saw Rabbit on my way home,"

said Franklin's father.

"He was playing a tin flute."

"I know," said Franklin. "I gave —"

"It was just like *my* old tin flute,"

said Franklin's father.

"It belonged to your grandpa."

"Uh-oh," said Franklin.

"I am going to go look for it,"

said Franklin's father.

"I am going to go look for Rabbit,"

said Franklin.

Franklin found Rabbit in the sandbox.

He gave him his marble.

"I need my tin flute back,"

said Franklin.

"It was my grandpa's."

"Sorry, Franklin,"
said Rabbit.
"I traded it to Bear
for his pail
and shovel."

"Oh, no!"
cried Franklin.
"I have to find Bear!"

Franklin and Rabbit found Bear

at the pond.

Rabbit gave Bear his pail and shovel.

"I need my tin flute back,"

said Franklin.

"It was his grandpa's," said Rabbit.

"Sorry, Franklin," said Bear.

"I traded it to Goose for her sailboat."

"Oh, no!" cried Franklin.

"I have to find Goose!"

Franklin and Rabbit and Bear

found Goose in the library.

"Are you sure?" asked his father.

Franklin reached

for the tin flute.

Tweak! Toot! Twack!

"Oh, yes," said Franklin.

"I'm sure."

32